AF239896

Wilfried Kriese

HALF-TIME
To Turn One's Weaknesses
Into One's Strengths

Wilfried Kriese
Mauer Verlag
Layout: Mauer Verlag
Cover illustration: Foto Faiss Rottenburg
translation of the German edition
first published through Mauer Verlag in 2001
Edition Wilfried Kriese 2017
First edition 2003

www.mauerverlag.de
www.wilfried-Kriese.de

ISBN: 9783868124941

The motto of Mauer Verlag since 1992
"Everybody wants to tear down some wall in their lives."

Inhalt

FOREWORD

In 1991, being only 27 years old, I published my autobiography. That is to say: only a part of it. For on the one hand, I lacked the courage to write in detail about my life since I did not want to publicly praise or criticize the people around me. On the other hand, I just lacked the courage to write about myself. Besides, there was not so much to write about then. Furthermore, I was not sure how much I wanted to reveal about myself. Obviously, a biography is something deeply personal.

When I wrote my first biography, I was, as I mentioned, just 22 years young, and you do not normally write a biography at that age. You do that when you are 60 or 70, after having accomplished something in life. Generally, only those people will write and, above all, publish their life's story, who have accomplished something special in terms of career. Usually this group of people will include politicians, athletes, actors, scientists, musicians, etc. But why should that be the case actually? Are not the lives of people from certain social backgrounds sometimes as interesting as those of famous people?

In the chapter "Extracts from My Life" from my first book Für die Behindertenintegration, ein direkt Betroffener informiert [For the Integration of the Disabled – Information by a Directly Affected Person], I wanted to prove that a person who had been given up from a psychological as well as medical perspective, and who therefore would have been confined to an institution for disabled people for the rest of his life, is well capable to develop the means to lead an independent life. I was in a position to point at myself as living proof. For in spite of all the doubts from some experts, integration did work out for me, and that was surely something to write about.

But then I asked myself why I should write a book, me, a former cognitively handicapped pupil who had been confined to a special school partly because of his weaknesses in the German language. I asked myself why I had actually learned to speak, read and write, and with utmost effort and difficulty at that. So I could cope better with life? Surely that was the prime reason at first. However, I was not satisfied with that one answer and this is how, thank God, my first book came into existence, a book which brought unexpected aspects into my life. Maybe it was also due to the fact that then my book was the first book by a former cognitively handicapped person, so that I found myself filling a gap.

After the publication of my first book and some political efforts, it became clear why somebody like me, however young, should not only write their biography but also publish it: for the people found that my way of addressing the public is more credible and authentic than some studied experts' lecturing about minorities. After publishing the book, I was totally overwhelmed by the quite favorable response I got from experts as well as from laymen. All this encouragement made me carry on despite my strong doubts and inferiority complexes. Many more books followed as well as political and social commitment, lectures and the foundation of my own publishing company. At the same time, I was taking adult evening classes in rhetoric, German and English, as well as several correspondence courses.

Of course, there was also my private life. I earned my living regularly and in 1988 I married my wife, who has been a great advisor to me to this very day. Oh well, and since this is the proper thing to do for a Suabian married couple, we bought an old apartment that needed renovating.

As the years went by, I became more and more known. While at first only few perceived me on a regional level, I am on my way to national publicity today.

I never dreamt of getting that far before I started going public.

I am getting more and more positive letters and encouragement by people from the most varied social strata who want to express their admiration. Indeed, for many I have already become a "role model," a realization which virtually scares me. Me a role model? Am I actually living up to it? Do I deserve it?

Finally I realized that basically I am not doing anything else than many other people: I am trying to cope with life as well as I can with all my weaknesses. I am just lucky to have found something that brings extraordinary joy to me and which happens to be interesting to a part of the public.

Today I am referred to in the media as a self-made man and a successful person, which of course I am glad to hear. But what bothers me is that many of the people who crossed my path and who I got the chance to know, accomplish quite a lot, too, but do not receive real recognition. For it is hardly noteworthy when somebody who belongs to a minority group or who has a tough initial position in society, leads a so-called normal life, despite the fact that this can only be accomplished with a lot of effort and strength.

So I got to know a lot of people for whom I have deep respect, because it is harder to build up a civil life under tough conditions than to pursue a career without really feeling what actual accomplishment in life means.

So for me, too, many little things that are trivial for most people, have been indescribable obstacles that had to be overcome.

This is why in this detailed biography I want to give some examples of people who I met in the course of my life, who have accomplished pretty much considering their lives' circumstances, and who I therefore too regard as "successful persons."

So fortunately, my biography Half-Time, to Turn One's Weaknesses Into One's Strengths will additionally make sense to those people with their lives' half-time ahead of them or behind them, and help them find the courage to accept their own weaknesses and follow individual paths, so as to define the concept of "SUCCESS" anew.

For me success means "to turn one's weaknesses into one's strengths and to master one's own path of life."

I want to close this foreword with an essay by a pupil who went to school with me. I discovered the essay in an old school magazine. Thank God that as a Suabian one learns from early on that one must not throw away anything because one may want to use it some day.

Plans and wishes of a school-boy in the 9th grade for his life after school

After I finished school, I want to be trained as a car mechanic. Then I will buy myself a car, and I will also buy up old cars, fix them and sell them again. I will also fix my friends' cars, if they want me to. And later on, I will try to pass my final exam, so that in case I should enter the military, I can start right away to work in the garage.

Maybe I will be able to have my own garage and fix cars there. And when I have become master mechanic, I will also employ workers.

Later, when I have earned enough money, I will build myself a house and treat myself to a vacation and a hot sportscar, around 130 horsepower.
Then I'll be able to say: I'm fine.

This is how far I, too, had gotten after my training and I continue to have deep respect for somebody who has advanced that far. But I just was not able to find any rest, and so I simply carried on from there, if one can call that "simple"...

MY DEAR PARENTAL HOME

I have one brother and two sisters who were born two years apart from one another. So in 1963, 4x2 = myself, since I was the youngest of them. Just like my siblings, I was born in Schwenningen. Since my parents had already begun to construct a house in Bästenhardt near Mössingen in the district of Tübingen in late 1962, I only lived in Schwenningen for two years. In June 1963, we moved into our finished semi-detached house. This is where I was raised. Our neighborhood was a genuinely working class housing area consisting predominantly of apartment blocks. In our street, however, there were only semi-detached houses with garages and gardens. At the time, that was the dream of every Suabian with a low income.

In terms of citizenry, our family home was fully intact, just like millions of others, too. Our father was earning money as an electrician and our mother took care of the family's well-being. My three siblings were quite regularly developed children, who stepped out of line only once in a while, just as is usual with children.

One thing, however, which was not quite normal, or maybe it was, was that my father was a war victim. World War II had left him a souvenir. He was not able to move his left knee for the rest of his life. In other respects, too, war had severely damaged his health.

Oh well, and me, I was a healthy child, too, one all parents wish for. I had full sets of fingers and toes, my teeth were growing normally, which caused my parents many a sleepless night. And I learn to crawl, walk, talk, just like the other neighborhood children, and I was even blond and had blue eyes.

THE SHOCK

On March 25, 1965, my childhood, which had not even begun, changed abruptly. But on that dreadful day, the lives of my mother and my three siblings changed as well. Almost exactly 20 years after the end of World War II, my father died of the effects of his war injuries. From that day on, we did no longer belong to your normal, average family. A new and tough phase in our lives began. All of a sudden, my mother was left alone with four little children. But there was one good thing about it. Since my father had died of the consequences of his war injuries, we received a war orphan's allowance. This is why my mother was able to dedicate herself fully to caring for our well-being.

After my father died, I did not get a new father or some kind of father in the shape of uncles, as a substitute. I did not miss that either for my mother became a stand-in for the role of my father. To this day, I am still glad about that, for during my school years, I got to know many children who suffered because of their fathers. Later I often asked myself if men really are pigs after all, but as I got older I decided simply not to be a pig, and that settles the question for me.

From that moment on, my life was to be different compared to the lives of healthy children. My father's death caused a shock for me, which had the consequence that my so-called normal development suffered a setback. The language I had learned so far went dumb and did not come back for many years, and then quite inarticulate. My behavior, too, was disturbed. Today, however, I am convinced that a large part of my behavioral disturbance, as doctors and pedagogues called it, had not come about due to the shock alone, but because of the fact that a child who is not quite normal is likely to be met with laughter and scorn and exclusion, which may all too often cause aggression. It is alarming that even today it often happens that people who do not correspond to socially fixed norms are excluded. In my opinion, this a clear case of discrimination.

After our father's death, we got to understand how prejudiced a much too large part of the people is against a single woman and her children. Here, I would like to point to the fact that during the 60s and 70s it was not usual for a woman to be independent, as it is now. Only after all the divorces and Women's Lib did that become less unusual in the ensuing years.

Today I have deep respect for mothers who raise their children on their own and who do not enter a new partnership forcedly, maybe chasing an illusion called "family idyll." (Was there ever such a thing?) I had to witness the terrible consequences that this generally brought for children of my social background too many times. Even today among the divorced pairs that I know I can discern the hope that "surely everything will be better with the next partner." In my opinion, changing partners frequently will often cause more suffering on the part of the children than on the part of the grown-ups, and much damage will be done to the children's social life. But I do not want to condemn those who look for harmony through a relationship, since we all are striving for that after all.

Since the days my mental impairment began, I got to feel all kinds of prejudice against me. All too often I was categorized as an idiot. That happened in the most varied ways.
Although in my neighborhood I was tolerated simply as Wilfried with his peculiarities, and therefore, thank God, did not experience much disastrous discrimination, this does not mean that I was not the object of ridicule. For instance, as a child I had a friend called Andrea. Even as a 6 year-old that name was unpronounceable for

me. So I always called her Abaea. Almost every time I went to pick her up to go playing, her mother, as soon as she saw me, would cry out "Abaea come," laughing her head off. That hurt me terribly. Today I know that her mother never meant that as an insult or even an act of discrimination; she just behaved according to her kind.

But during my time in kindergarten, in school and in my apprenticeship, I often got to feel what it is like when other children were explicitly told not to make friends with people like me. Through these horrible experiences, I became aware of the fact that I was different from the other children. Later these experiences helped me tell a friend from a "friend".

MEMORIES OF A CLINICAL YOUTH HOSPITAL

When I was four years old, I was sent to the Clinical Youth Hospital of the Child Psychiatry in Tübingen for two months. There they examined where my mental disturbances came from, in order to determine their origin; although it was quite clear that from the moment of my father's death nothing in my mental development was normal anymore.

Today I ask myself if the doctors' task was to find out something which was already evident, or whether I was more of a guinea pig. Well, anyway, my staying in the clinical youth hospital became compulsory, as it were, since one important issue was which authority or department would pay my necessary treatment in the future.

Unfortunately in 1967 it was far from clear which authority, i.e. which department was obliged to pay for necessary treatment in a case like mine. At that point, far too little was being done for the handicapped. Improvements of all kinds for mentally and physically challenged children, adolescents, as well as grown-ups were not introduced before the 70s.

After much progress, many of the accomplishments are being annihilated today, something which politicians justify as social reforms. In health matters generally, much wrong is being done to needy patients. I often ask myself whether this current tendency can still be called normal or whether those who are responsible have simply gone mad. I get so overwhelmed with anger that I would like to forget my general non-violent attitude and punch some of them in the face. For, if one does not see a chance in the necessity of investing money in the future of the people who need support, one should not be surprised if more and more people become dependent on the welfare state. For success can only ensue if a person, regardless of their level of education, is properly supported.

When I entered the clinical youth hospital, I had to separate from my mother, my siblings and my usual surroundings for the first time.

The hospital had different groups. And as it was usually the case then – as it partly is now – boys and girls were separated. I had to share a dormitory with seven children, every child having their own mental disturbances. For me it was a nightmare to share the room with completely unknown people without any preparation. Furthermore, there were some children among them who were ready to do insane things. For instance, one of them was absolutely sure that he was able to fly, so that all the window handles had to be removed. Another had a tendency toward rebellion and would occasionally strike out wildly with his arms. The rest of the children, who were between 4 and 10 years old, were more or less behaviorally disturbed so that, being a child, I could not make out what was actually wrong with them.

Our daily routine was to get up early, wash, dress and to prepare for breakfast. After that we went to the kindergarten, which was situated on the hospital premises. There at least 30 to 40 children were taken care of by only one old kindergarten teacher. But nevertheless I liked going there because the teacher was incredibly gentle and obliging toward the children and always had a smile on her face.

At noon, we had lunch. After that we had to take a nap for around 2 hours. I can well remember that these two hours were a nightmare for me because there was no way I could fall asleep. After that nap, we were kept busy and analyzed by the pedagogues in our group until dinner. After dinner a nursery teacher told us a good night's story (television was not very widespread then). And then it was lights out.

We were not allowed to plan our day ourselves; or rather, the daily routines were dictated to us every day anew. Since my stay in the hospital included loads of examinations, probably for the other children as well, my homesickness was not the only unpleasant thing.

There was one examination which I can recall so well today that it seems to have taken place just an hour ago. One morning, while I was still in my pajamas, I was taken by two nurses to an examination room next to the dormitory. There I received, for whatever reasons, several injections directly into my back and my spinal column. For the first time in my life I learned what real pain is. Since I was screaming like mad, all the children came to see what the matter was. They kept watching through a glass pane until they were chased away by the staff. If I remember well, I was not able to get up after this examination for three days because of the pain in my back. Every time I tried to get up from my bed, I immediately broke down screaming with terrible, stabbing pain.

During the two months, there were countless examinations that only proved to the doctors and authorities what had been evident from the first: that my speech defect as well as my behavioral disturbance had been caused by a shock, my father's death.

THERAPEUTIC EXPERIENCES

In order to treat the effects of my shock, I underwent therapy in Tübingen from 1968 to 1969. Due to the fact that my mother did not have a car, we went to Tübingen by train twice a week. Since my siblings had to be taken care of first, my mother was always in a hurry to get to the station in Belsen 2 kilometers away. Although we were not in danger of missing the train, we had to cross the gate in time in order to reach the station. And that was something. In those times, there were no "gate wards" yet, who would let the gate down on the side of the road with a crank before the arrival of the train. And those who did not make it to the other side of the tracks in time, would miss their train. And since the gate ward sometimes worked according to her own schedule, she occasionally let down the gate ten minutes too early. Fortunately, the gate came down very slowly and the ringing was so loud that it signaled to all the pedestrians to walk a little faster.

I can well remember that my mother used to walk through Tübingen as fast as possible, or even run, since there often were political demonstrations that were taking place in all the other university towns, too, during the movement of '68. And since my mother was only getting the worst picture about these demonstrations through the media, she was afraid like hell to run into some act of violence. So I had my first experiences with media neurosis through my own mother. I realized that years later, however; then I was just annoyed by her dragging me through Tübingen by the hand.

Every therapeutic session had a length of roughly 2 hours. I was always looking forward very much to these hours because the young therapist who took care of me would be very obliging to me and had a more than natural and kind way about her. The treatment went on as follows: My pronunciation was trained through various games so that one could understand me at least a little better. My imagination would be so stimulated by this that about half a year later I could decide myself what games to play with the therapist; that helped me build up my self-confidence. Since the session took place while I was still in kindergarten, they also helped me cope with my kindergarten group better.

However, the fact that I was allowed to decide what I wanted to play had consequences. And the fact that my therapist just could not refuse me a wish was to be the reason for her transfer. For one day I decided to play doctors and nurses. And since, as I suspect now, she was a little too much influenced by the spirit of the movement of '68, the game ended with the session being over before I was done with my examinations, and I left the room without my therapist. When my mother asked where the woman was, I answered that she was almost naked. One can certainly imagine the rest. My mother was so upset that she immediately went to complain to some professor so that we, as a consequence, missed our train, something I could perfectly live with however. But the fact that I was not to see my therapist again from that moment on, although she certainly had not done anything bad, ruined the joy I felt at the sessions.

After the treatment was completed, I went to Tübingen for language therapy for half a year; there my speech defects were tackled with great success and more intensely than they had been by the general therapeutic treatment.

Although most of the doctors were of the opinion that the language lessons were useless in my case anyway, my mother could not be deterred by these learned charlatans from taking me to language therapy nevertheless. Which was a good thing, because by the time I started school my pronunciation had become a lot better. For instance, I was now able to pronounce my name, which I had not been able before when I would say, for example, Wiffied instead of Wilfried and bidday instead of birthday, etc.

On top of the clever commentaries of a lot of doctors, the health service refused to pay the various treatments that were connected to my shock. Only when my mother put them under pressure and threatened to talk to the press in case they did not pay, the officials began to judge the situation correctly, and the understood that when my mother threatened to do something, she was certainly going to carry out that threat.

So I often saw how very energetic and aggressive my mother could become. What I was not conscious of, as a child, is that without her restless efforts I would now be living and working in a home for disabled people.

I got to know a lot of people who were struck by that fate because experts had simply taken the wrong decisions. This shows that much can be achieved when weak and handicapped people are given the right support and treatment. And on the other hand, money that is invested in support and education can be regained many times over if many an allegedly hopeless case was allowed to live an integrated life.

During the most severe period of my illness, most authorities, doctors, etc. agreed that a mental home would be the best for me. Well, fortunately my mother had not listened to these educated ladies and gentlemen. Instead, I was able to develop into a healthy, self-confident and inquisitive person in the following years. But before I got there, there still were a lot of walls to climb over.

KINDERGARTEN

When I was four years old, after some examinations and advice from experts whether I should go at all to kindergarten or rather be shut up in an institution for handicapped people, I was sent to a kindergarten in Belsen, about 2 kilometers from my parental home, thanks to my mother's efforts.

It was extremely difficult then to find a place in a regular kindergarten for a child like me, since, in those times, children who corresponded so little or even less to the norm than I did either entered the handicapped home circuit right away or else had to be taken care of by their parents without any educational or public support. The reason was that society was not yet adjusted to the idea of integration at all. If politics had cared about that issue at the time of, say, the German economic boom after World War II, many handicapped people and their families would have been spared a lot of unnecessary trouble, and there would be significantly more handicapped or retarded people today living an integrated life while contributing as much to society as everybody else.

Thanks to the commitment of a lot of parents and pedagogues, it is considerably easier today to get handicapped or retarded children into a regular kindergarten. Unfortunately, even nowadays there are still too many parents who are opposed to the idea of integrating children with mental or physical handicaps into regular kindergartens. Today I feel nothing but pity and contempt for these parents.

Well anyway, I was sent to a kindergarten with healthy children and was of course looked after along with them. The kindergarten consisted of a group of about 40 children. In those times, there was not yet a full educational program as it is offered today in an often exaggerated manner. The day started with us children taking seats on chairs arranged in a big circle and singing some songs. After that, the kindergarten teacher, who, judging from her age, had already been trained as a kindergarten teacher during the war, would tell us a story. We would then form groups and play with some toys. The only thing the kindergarten teacher would do then was to sit on a chair at one side of the room seeing to it that nobody got too loud. And if someone did step out of line once in a while, she would be quick to give the kid a good hiding.

I never belonged to any group so I was just my own playmate. I would simply invent a comrade and his dog and would play and talk to them in complete silence. Since I had to face exclusion from the very beginning of my childhood, the other children, too, often made me feel that I was different from them, which was a hard thing to cope with. Although there was a lot that, due to my childlike mind, I was not able to comprehend intellectually, I often was very painfully affected emotionally.

On some occasions, it was brutally brought home to me that I was suffering from a speech defect. I can remember an instance so well as if it had happened only recently. There was a combine harvester which would drive past the kindergarten once in a while, and when we kids were playing outside we would run to the fence and would shout out the word "combine harvester" several times in a row as loud as we could. For me, however, that word was unpronounceable and so I just shouted "ata ata ata..." as loud as I could, which would of course cause great amusement so that the kids would laugh at me from the top of their voices. At that time I did not understand that the kids were not being mean; it was just childlike behavior without actually unkind thoughts. But the fact that the kindergarten teacher never seriously intervened just shows the amount of understanding there was for children of my kind.

Over a year later, I was sent to a kindergarten which had opened recently and which was only a few hundred yards away from my parents' home. So everything started again. I was being laughed at and had to adapt as well as it was possible in those times. This time around, however, I was already prepared and was able to get used to that kindergarten faster than the last one. Still I was not spared the feeling of being different from the others. But this time I was at least able to find some comrades that I could get along with. So I could say farewell to my old imaginary friend and his dog (a collie). At last I had some kids who liked to be with me even during their leisure time. It was of great help that the kindergarten teachers were significantly more progressive educators than my teacher in Belsen. They showed a lot of understanding toward me and settled many a conflict among the group that came about because of my behavior or even my sheer presence. But what deeply hurt emotionally was not the question whether more kids wanted to play with me, but their screwed-up parents who behaved as if I had a fatal, catching disease. And apart from that, I was from a fatherless family.

Unfortunately, I did not only experience discrimination by young and old people during my time in kindergarten, which would certainly have been enough, but had to confront prejudices during my whole childhood, adolescence, and still have to today.

LANGUAGE TRAINING

In order to be treated correctly and intensely for my speech defect, I was sent to a speech therapy school in Sondelfingen near Reutlingen for half a year in 1973, when I was 10 years old. That of course was a great change for me. For on the one hand I had to leave the school I was used to and had to befriend new kids, which did not work because, as my home town was relatively far away, I could not see them during leisure time. On the other hand, the bus ride had to be endured.

My new school was at almost 30 kilometers' distance from my home town. I had to cover that distance by bus which went from Belsen to Reutlingen. There I had to change the bus at the station which was pretty intricate for a ten-year old. With all the rushed activity there, I felt like a confused dwarf. I had to get used to that first so my mother went with me a couple of times. She showed me what I had to do in case I should happen to miss the bus. After some time I actually managed to master the long daily distance all by myself.

In order to kill some time during the long bus ride, I slowly began to get into reading. I loved to devour comic books which were somewhat violent in their style and not particularly valuable pedagogically either. When my new teacher discovered what I was reading, he was shocked and wanted to make me read different magazines and books. But his reading recommendations were as appealing to me as an old rotten apple. So after some time he wanted to have a talk with my mother. He tried to convince her to make me, who was also present, stop reading these magazines by all means. My mother, however, told him that she was certainly not going to do that since she was quite happy that I was reading at all, and with a lot of enthusiasm even; and that if one forced me to read something that did not interest me, I very probably would not read anything at all. So I learned to read through comic books.

A couple of months after, I wanted to know where the little babies came from. Since in those times it was a taboo to talk about that with one's children, and since it was not yet usual for teachers in elementary school to do that for the parents, my mother bought me my first biology book for kids with a lot of color illustrations, which I would eagerly read on my way to school. That was the first book in my life.

The syllabus in my new school was designed after that of a usual elementary school. Since I had not yet come across such subjects at my old school, I was in trouble of course. The teachers, however, did not pay too much attention to that, since the classes were designed especially for kids with speech defects and handicaps and that was the prime reason I was there anyway.

In class, we worked a lot with a tape recorder. Every single girl and boy had their own recorder. I was particularly proud of mine. None of my siblings, or anybody else among my friends had their own tape recorder then.

The recorder served to help us to better control our pronunciation; it was always running during our speech exercises so we could then play the tape back and listen to our own pronunciation. As a consequence, I was able to improve my language feel.

In addition to the tape recorder method, I got individual classes twice a week, where my speech defects were tackled through special learning methods. By means of some kind of sign language (one sign for every letter) I got the feel for every new word I learned on a practical level.

Since I often got sick during the bus rides and since the way to school was too long for me, I went back to my old, familiar school after about six months. What made me glad in particular was that I was finally going to be able to be with my old classmates again, during and after classes.

SONDERSCHÜLER SUPPENTRIELER

"Sonderschüler Suppentrieler [= a kid who goes to a special school for the handicapped and who allegedly cannot drink soup without spilling it) goes to school and can't do anything," how many times did I have to hear that verse sung!

After some aptitude tests as well as some advice given to my mother, they decided that I should not go to elementary school like all the other kindergarten kids, but to the special school for children with learning difficulties in Mössingen.

My first school day was in 1971. Since the decision which school to put me in had taken some time, I entered after the current term had already begun. It was during the time when schools of this kind were being established all over West Germany, so that parents had hardly a chance to register their handicapped kids at a usual school, since that application would simply be denied with reference to the fact that there was now a new kind of school for the handicapped instead. Today I think that this was both good and bad since many kids like me might have been overstretched in a usual school. Many children, however, who would have been in good hands with intermediate school, maybe with some supplementary courses, were put in special schools for children with learning difficulties instead. And because of the introduction of that kind of school, there was little interest on the part of the educational system to support weak or handicapped children within the context of an intermediate school.

I do not know how many times my mother went with me to the most varied elementary schools to check whether I might go to a usual school. But I simply was not suited to this kind of school. I can still recall when my mother went with me to a special school to ask for advice. Although there were no more than 20 kids, they could only spare a little side room at a Mössingen fire station for them, while there certainly would have been an empty room for them on the premises of the intermediate and secondary school nearby. But in those times, kids of my kind were not exactly desired. The situation of handicapped and educationally subnormal people was generally discriminating. Often, handicapped kids would not even go to school, something the school board was not particularly concerned by either. So there was something good about the special schools for handicapped people since at least they provided those children and adolescents who did not conform to the norm with an access to education.

I can recall very well that I was looking forward to my first school day with great excitement. I would have loved to get a big cone full of sweets, but since the term had already begun and I would have attracted a little too much attention, I found a multicolored plate with all kinds of sweets and toys on the breakfast table.

At least the school for kids with learning difficulties already had a classroom of its own at the intermediate school when I entered school. The first four classes were taught at this class comprehensively. At the end of my second school year, my special school even got its own school building. Stupid as it may seem, the school was constructed on a little hill on the middle of the Mössingen school premises surrounded by the intermediate school, the secondary school and high school. Although it made sense in terms of integration, it seemed absurd to place a little building whose architecture attracted attention anyway upon a hill. So not only were we already considered as outsiders, but anybody who did not know the Mössingen school premises would immediately ask what that funny building on the hill was all about. This has not changed to this day.

In the course of my school years the number of pupils rose to about 140 so that the school building had to expanded. But ironically, our school was attached to the high school building and so problems were created for us which gave us a hard time. If something occurred on the school premises, they were most likely to blame us. We were certainly no angels, and some of my classmates were known for their practical jokes even all over Mössingen. But in the end we got very upset to be again and again accused of things we had not done, and since we never got any apology whatsoever, even when our innocence had been confirmed, we realized that we were playing the role of scapegoats.

But apart from that I felt safe and at home at the special school. Since all the school children had some kind of learning difficulty, there were hardly any prejudices among us; we were all in the same boat. Also, the teachers were very progressive and pedagogical idealists in those times and did not hesitate to sacrifice a considerable share of their free time to give additional private lessons.

In our fifth grade we even had a teacher who was very strict and whom we would simply call "Asshole," but who was an outstanding pedagogue and who even succeeded in having handicapped kids transferred to intermediate school for the first time. It was a unique accomplishment on the part of the pupils as well as the teacher, who had equipped them with the necessary prerequisites. I still have deep respect for any teacher who enables their pupils to take such a leap.

Outside school the whole matter of good will as well as safety looked completely different. Most of my classmates had as much difficulty making friends with other groups as I had, so that outside school I could only establish a small circle of friends where I was accepted as I was. So it did not come as a surprise that after class we kids from the special school would gather in small gangs that had not the best of reputation. But we stuck together like glue because we respected one another. Surely we had our losers who we would play tricks on, but even they were never excluded and were able to find a group where they belonged.

At this school I guess I made some progress in learning and in the course of time my speech defect got better, too, with speech therapy school playing an important role.

But the greatest difficulty was that I was a dyslexic so that I could relatively cope with most subjects except when it came to reading and writing. Math was not one of my strengths either so that I did not particularly like that school. And since I would occasionally freak out if something was not going my way or could not deal with some conflicts I had, I would sometimes just skip school. This went on until the fifth grade. Then I got the teacher we called "Asshole," but who excellently held me in check in his own way.

My mother did everything to get me the education that I needed for advancement so she would never hesitate to pay for private lessons. Since we were not exactly rich, I was lucky to have teachers who would give me private lessons once or twice a week at cost price. Without these teachers I would not have received a lot of help, which I urgently needed. I realize the importance of these idealistic teachers not only when looking at myself but also at some of my classmates who, although they had severe learning problems, succeeded in passing the final exams in intermediate school and would even learn a profession which would later provide for themselves and even their own families.

But unfortunately despite strong support, I also saw many classmates of mine becoming criminals and ending up in prison.

When we were in the third and fourth grade, we would very often have fights with kids from other schools. The reason was that we all felt we were outsiders and, indeed, we were. I hardly fought myself because I just was not the type and was much too feeble besides. I remained a feeble boy all the way into adolescence and did certainly not come across as very frightening. Furthermore, I had not known violence at home, in contrast to some of my classmates who came from homes where they were being literally abused. Of course kids and adolescents from other schools, too, have had that background. But if one comes from a disrupted home where one gets to experience a good hiding regularly, maybe sexual abuse, and other kinds of aversion; and if one happens to belong to a minority which is repudiated by other people, one is likely to react towards society with violence.

I often observe today that people who get annoyed by members of such minority groups become horrified and begin to cry for the police. They speak in a condescending manner of these young and old rebels without realizing that that is the very reason why there are more and more cases of assault and battery, for instance. But politicians who run down these people who I, too, once belonged to, make me want to clench my fists and punch their faces. In these situations, some repressed anger rises within me, but I have learned to handle it through the years. So I opt against violence but for meaningful dialog instead, so that this sort of politician and their voters get to be unmasked as pure charlatans.

Some of my classmates in whose homes a good beating was as natural as saying grace was with other families, were absolutely hardened against pain and violence. I can still recall very well when during a swimming course in the seventh grade our physical education teacher asked one of my classmates, who knew daily beating at home, about the shockingly distinct welts on his back.

To this the boy answered as casually as if he was saying that his father had given him 10 euros, that his father whipped him with a belt.

At the end of the eighth grade we were asked where which job we would like to take later on. For me it was clear that I wanted to be an animal keeper. I have always been crazy about animals. Even as a child I was interested in the care and the behavior of all sorts of animals. From the fifth grade on I was especially into aquariums and they have remained a passion ever since. So it was pretty obvious for me to do a practical course at a pet shop. But although one day the advisors talked me out of that wish, I was determined to study really hard so that one day I could get the job of my dreams. But I never got there.

Learning was tough in the ninth grade since our teacher made us prepare for our final exams at intermediate school with great strictness and determination. My God, how I despised her then, I felt I needed her like a hole in the head. Twenty years later during a lecture in her class, while they were shooting a TV documentary about me, I was asked by a pupil whether I liked that teacher and at first I did not know what to answer, but then I replied: "No, I didn't like her at all, but today I know that she is a very good teacher and that I owe my graduation to her." What I did not say was that it was this teacher who had sacrificed hours of her free time to help me prepare for my finals.

For us special school pupils, the passing of our final exams was as great an achievement as graduation was for a high school student. Although I barely made it through the exam, my joy was indescribable. And out of 17 pupils a full 15 passed the exam. It was not just a success for us, but for our teacher, too. This is why I think that teachers in particular have a rather thankless job, for only years later can they tell if they have been successful. In that respect, even writing a book is easier, since the results can be seen after a relatively short time and one has got something to show. But before I got there, there were still some stony roads before me.

LET´S GO FIND A JOB

In 1979 I finished the special school with a intermediate school degree. Since an apprenticeship as an animal keeper was ruled out, I started out by participating in a year-long program for vocational orientation at the IBS (International Association für Sozialarbeit, International Federation for Social Work). The purpose of that year was to help the participants get used to a regular working day routine and, additionally, to get a better orientation professionally. One could to choose four out of six lines of profession, carpentry, metalwork, housekeeping, horticulture, painting and bricklaying, that one would be working in for six weeks each in the first six months. I picked metalwork, housekeeping, painting and carpentry. For the remaining six months, the participants could settle for one line of profession in order to get introduced to it on a more practical level and to get more discipline. That was certainly necessary considering the coarse behavior of many boys and girls who would hardly been able to cope with a regular vocational training straight after school.

I settled for carpentry. It was rather fascinating for me to work with wood because one can make just anything out of wood ranging from a small wooden figure to an elaborate closet. Even today I love to do carpentry.

At the IBS I lived in a home for boys that was situated in the same area as the workshops and the home for girls. So it was just a matter of time until I fell in love with a girl and had my first intense experiences with the female sex. Since all the adolescent participants were in a critical age, the educators who were in charge had to keep an eye on the couples in particular. But that did not only involve severe consequences. For instance, the girls were not allowed to be in the boys' rooms, nor were the boys were not allowed to be in the girls' rooms. If one did not follow that regulation, one could face expulsion. But although some couples were occasionally caught in the act, it never came to that. Instead, some educators took precautionary measures right from the start and, together with the adolescents, arranging several evenings that were dedicated to talk about friendship and sexuality in an frank manner. We also learned about methods of contraception and where one could get the various contraceptives. We were even given condoms and vaginal suppositories. So there was only one girl during that whole years who got pregnant.

I shared my room with my friend with whom I had gone to school. Our room was on the ground floor. The rooms there were much craved for by some inhabitants of the home, since there was a curfew after the doors were shut at 10 p.m., it was rather inviting for some to sneak out of the window on the ground floor. I cannot recall how many times I heard someone knocking at the door or the window in the middle of the night because they had their nightly adventure before or behind them.

In the IBS there were only adolescents or young grown-ups who had gone to a special school for children with learning difficulties or had not been very good in intermediate school. Altogether there were 120 girls and boys in the workshops, among them 20 external people who were not accommodated in the home. Since the participants very different almost everybody could find a group where they would feel at ease. That made that year quite bearable for me.

There was a boy at our boarding school who was physically handicapped and a little behaviorally disturbed. In short, he was obviously different from us and initially had trouble making contact and finding acceptance. But as the months went by, he participated more and more in the daily activities at the boarding school and the workshops, so that we boys and girls not only got to tolerate but to accept him. He integrated into the group so well that one could see that he felt at ease and that he was one of us; and all this despite the fact that, according to the pedagogical experiences of those times, he would have belonged in an institution for handicapped people.

The weekly routine for us adolescents who were in the carpentry workshop ran as follows. On Mondays and Tuesdays we had classes in the morning and went to the workshop in the afternoon. On Wednesday we spent the whole day in the workshop. On Thursday all the participants, of the other workshops, too, went to trade school in the IBS buildings. On Fridays we would work until noon before the weekend began.

Classes were not different from the usual trade schools classes. There were four school classes with the most different teachers. Among them, there was an asshole, too, but I was glad we had him; today I have the impression that he had come from a so-called androposophic school. His classes were just fun. When the subject matter had been demanding or boring, he was very good at turning classes interesting again by means of informal projects, such as producing a funny radio play which he would record on tape with us, or reading Asterix comic books. With this he was able to reach the maladjusted boys and girls, of whom there were quite a lot.

I had a classmate in trade school who was particularly interested in social issues and especially in the books by Günter Wallraff. He was so committed to the journalistic work Wallraff was doing at the time that he was even allowed to give classes on that on his own. We watched videofilms about Wallraff's work and also looked at his career. This got me more and more interested in social issues and politics during my year there. It stirred a passion which has endured to this day.

On Fridays at noon, some of the internal inhabitants were allowed to go home for the weekend. Although the weekdays were quite bearable for me, I was very glad to come home to my usual surroundings. The few people who were not capable of going home because the trip would have been too long or too expensive – they could only go home once every four weeks, since the employment office would pay one trip home per month – were offered varied possibilities to spend their leisure time. During the week, too, there was so much going on that in comparison TV is as interesting as the President's speech on Sundays.

Since I rather liked working with wood, I picked, more or less consciously, the profession of wood workman, because I had been told from early on that I could not hope to be trained as an animal keeper.

TRAINEE YEARS

Your time as a trainee is a hard time. That saying has hit the nail on the head for me.

Like I said, since I could not be trained as an animal keeper, I opted for an apprenticeship as a wood workman while I was at the program for vocational orientation. After all, everybody said that it was beautiful to work with wood.

When in September 1980 I started my 3 year apprenticeship as a professional wood workman at the 'Haus am Berg' in Bad Urach, I realized it all of a sudden. In my school years I had already worked in a wood factory in order to increase my pocket money. Now, however, I became conscious of the fact that this existence as a factory worker was going to be my life's work. I could not put up with that because I did not like the atmosphere in the factory hall right from the start.

The profession of wood workman requires special training for three years where the apprentices learn exactly the same as in the case of wood technician or wood mechanic but with the essential difference that at the end one does not receive a journeyman's diploma but just a leaving certificate. This is why this profession cannot be seen as equivalent as wood technician or wood mechanic. For instance, as a wood workman one cannot get a master craftsman's diploma and this means that this training is a dead end street. Of course there is the possibility of do additional training but that would take two more years in a factory.

Now, it is easy to imagine that an apprentice who has finally finished his three years of training will hardly feel like adding two more years. But of course it is important that I also mention that for many who learn this profession it is a good opportunity to be able to at least show one job qualification. Because to have a special school diploma without any further training means that one will remain an unskilled worker for the rest of one's life, and this will certainly not improve one's self-confidence.

I know that some former apprentices were able to advance further after finishing their special training, so that they either continued as carpenters or even learned a new profession.
There were 10 apprentices trained at the wood workshop in 'Haus am Berg,' and all of them had to cope with more or less severe learning difficulties. All the apprentices took necessary supplementary courses in the special trade school on the premises of 'Haus am Berg.' So it was made sure that everyone passed their final exam.

Since 'Haus am Berg' is an institution for handicapped people with appended workshops, with about 130 mentally and physically handicapped people working there when I was there, I started to seriously deal with the issue of being handicapped.

At that time I spent a lot of time with a relatively severely handicapped person I liked to work with and with whom I spent my breaks. At first some fellow apprentices used to sneer at that, but it was not long before they accepted it. I tried to be his comrade outside 'Haus am Berg' as well. Every time I went home on Friday, I sat beside him. Since this was not a special bus for the transportation of handicapped people but a usual city bus, it was not my comrades but some of the passengers that looked at me, because nobody would sit beside the handicapped person from 'Haus am Berg' except maybe for an elderly passenger who could not find another free seat.

The apprentices directly lived downtown in the home for apprentices. I was not only pissed off because of the factory work but because of the home, too. This certainly had to do with the fact that, after my time at the IBS, I was being kept from my usual surroundings for three more years. But I also had problems living together with other people; that made those three years even harder. I was an active and dynamic person even then, and since most of the inhabitants were less active and predominantly watched TV, I found myself in an environment where I did not particularly feel at ease. But my relations with some apprentices evolved into solid comradeship, and in one case virtually into friendship. That friendship has lasted to this day.

Without the educators I would probably not have finished my apprenticeship. I still have comradely relations with one of them and I try to see him at least once a year.

Since, compared to the IBS, the range of possible leisure activities was absolutely meager due to lack of interest, I decided to join a sports club at the beginning of my second year as apprentice in order to take to martial arts, which had long fascinated me. Since there was a lot of prejudice against the inhabitants of 'Haus am Berg,' that step was not that easy to take for me. But my doubts turned out to be unfounded. Although my fellow club members knew that I was at 'Haus am Berg,' they accepted me in spite of initial skepticism. But nevertheless I had to deal with their frequently making quite derisive, indeed, insulting remarks about the handicapped people at 'Haus am Berg.'

One day while I was training, my left kneecap sprang out. As a consequence, I had to be operated three times, and have been suffering from it ever since. The only advantage I got from it was that I became unfit for military service. Since I was going to refuse military service anyway, I did not regret that.

Due to that accident I had to miss some classes, but I was able to improve my average because I generally did not find learning particularly difficult. I could improve my results in every subject, except for grammar. But at the same time I was making much progress in reading, so that I turned into a bookworm.

Although I was getting on at trade school, my attitude toward factory work did not change. The reason was that the apprenticeship focussed on turning the apprentices into good and productive engineers. I was absolutely unable to picture myself earning my living by operating some roaring machine for the rest of my life. But I pulled through it nevertheless, hoping that with it there would arise opportunities I could profit from in my future career.

Since I dealt with handicapped people more and more during those three years, I could not get rid of the suspicion that many handicapped people are inexplicably put in institutions despite the fact that, given a certain support, they could live their lives in a fully or almost fully autonomous manner if they were only this society showed more consideration for them.

Because of my close contact with the handicapped at 'Haus am Berg,' I thought about becoming a professional educator after finishing my apprenticeship. But as I realized that an educator can hardly do anything about the current situation of the handicapped because he has to subordinate himself to the authorities' as well as the institutions' guidelines and regulations, no matter how sensible, absolutely stupid or even inhuman they may be, I decided against that profession.

In August 1983, the time had finally come: I successfully concluded my apprenticeship. Now a part of my life began which did not take place in some sheltered institution; here was the serious life.

THE SERIOUS LIFE

I had hardly finished my apprenticeship when it was already time to enter the factory. I was as much looking forward to that as a postman looks forward to a vicious dog that is already after his bottom.

This kind of work was a big disappointment for my professional start because I realized how ruthlessly a company can be run by playing off workers against each other in order to increase production. After two weeks of getting familiar with my work, they made me work directly at an assembly line where kitchen units were being joined together in quick succession. The pay left a lot to be desired, despite the great amount of work that was being expected. Since the inhuman conditions in that company pissed me off, I left after about five weeks.

At that time, politics was proclaiming "More Future Through Productivity." So I naturally wondered how a person must be feeling who, try as they might, cannot live up to such a system of pressure, or who feels like a worker who is so dependent on money that he sees no other possibility than to let himself be exploited. So I was less and less surprised at the fact that a weaker person will be pulled to pieces, because if one cannot handle one's own weaknesses and helplessness, a scapegoat will probably be needed.

I have had to make that observation in my everyday work life again and again; except that today I work no longer in the factory, where allegedly there are only so-called uneducated people employed, but at the university, and there that behavior is much more pronounced. By now I have come to the conclusion that the more educated people are, the more mean and envious the can be.

Two weeks after I had left, I had an operation on my knee due to the effects of my sports accident. As a consequence, I became unemployed and of course got thrown behind financially, too, because I had been able to make small payments to my unemployment insurance. And that is when I made my next life experience, namely, how all of a sudden one can drop in social hierarchy. But I was still lucky because I was still living with my mother. After four months of rest, my knee was better so that I could put myself to work again.

I decided to earn some money in order to make a trip through Europe by train. I earned it working temporarily at a plastic factory. I did not like it at all. For hours on end I had to remove plastic units from machines every 2 to 3 minutes. After a while one starts to count the seconds out of sheer boredom and that can make a working day seem never-ending. But I could cope with it because I knew that after four months, with some money and a duffel bag, I would be able to make a two month tour.

These two months did more to my self-confidence than my whole time at school and as an apprentice. I set out without any knowledge about the countries. When I was in Spain I met some Norwegians who were on their way to Portugal. After the two of them had told me about that country, I decided to join them. But where the hell was Portugal actually, I did not have a clue, and since I did not want to make a fool of myself, I bought a map in Barcelona to find out.

During that trip through Europe I got to know the most varied people, cultures and life styles. Due to the fact I was left to my own devices for the first time and had to make all decisions myself, but also had to organize my finances and look for a bed for the night myself, I gained a lot of self-confidence. I realized that I was not stupid at all. During that time I slept in youth hostels, on beaches, in cheap boarding houses and, if there was none such possibility, I even slept on park benches among homeless people. That was when I really go to know that kind of people and I decided that I never would end up like this. Today I feel pretty close to the homeless, for I know how easily you can get there. You lose your job, you have hardly saved any money, unemployment benefits expire, and then life only has to deal out one of its vicissitudes, for instance, an important person dies, before you will end up sleeping on the park bench.

Back home I had to present myself at the employment office. And there I had to make a further crackpot experience. I was allowed to volunteer for construction work where there was some really hard work involved. I was being forced with money, for if I had not cooperated they would have cut off unemployment benefits. The consequences were clear, my knee got worse and I had to break off construction work after four months. But if that was not enough, my second operation was due and kept me off work again for some time. Now one might want to ask, well, why did this Kriese not look for another job? The reason was that I had to wait to have my medical examination for military service and no employer would take the risk to hire me. For in case of a draft order, the job would have had to be kept vacant. But since the unemployment rate was very high then and the employers did not know what the market conditions were going to be like after a year or two, they preferred to employ other young men instead.

After that I worked for a short time in a plastic factory where I was dismissed because of my bad knee. I found that work excellent because in the context of plastic model making I could prepare molds, and that was more than interesting.

At the end of 1985, I was hired as a painter in a wood company. I worked there for three years. Since I was often ill because of my knee and had to have two more operations, some people working at the company as well as others often made me appear to be lazy. Now, apart from having to face the reactions to my special school and job training background, I got to feel what it is like not to be able to physically function the way our society expects it. So I was fed up with jobs where respect and comradeship depends on output. This is why in 1986 I decided to turn my back on factory work and to earn my living through a job that would be more satisfying, even if that meant less pay.

At a Christmas party in 1988 the boss I had then made rather insulting and very hurtful remarks about my special job training as well as my time in special school: "As to you I guess I've been had; if I had known about the kind of apprenticeship you had, I wouldn't have hired you." But that was not all, he said something even stupider: "Had I known what kind of school you went to, I wouldn't have hired you either." I had to listen to that after my time at special school had been over for almost 10 years. Although I reacted to some of his discriminating gibberish, I was too bitter about his opinions and I just could not be bothered to keep talking to him about that.

Two weeks after that conversation, I found a new job at the University of Tübingen as a caretaker for the premises and laboratories. And so I made new working experiences because when, as a hot-headed young man, one switches from factory to a public institution, i.e. university, one realizes that they are really worlds apart.

Since I had no connections to the state it was a matter of luck to get a job there at all. Or was it? I was doing a kind of work hardly any other German would do, namely emptying the garbage cans at a chemistry institute. For this kind of work I virtually had the ideal qualifications.

In February 1989 I had my first workday at the University of Tübingen. I did not mind at all that I was only in charge of the garbage. For me it was simply a chance to escape factory work so I could at last develop more freely. Besides I thought, at least I am working for the state, and some day I will certainly find something else. For I knew that if you work for the state you have fixed working hours, without constantly having to work overtime, which takes up a lot of valuable leisure time, and that there is no piecework.

But I could not know that a university really has its own rules. While my past work life had required effort and ideas for improvement, the reverse was the case now. What I had to learn most was that you had better not contradict the doctors and professors and other superiors and that you had better follow all instructions no matter how wrong they may be. I understood as much after three years, but I still cannot keep to it because then I would have to puke if I looked in the mirror. An attitude like this will of course cause a lot of trouble.

Due to some organizational changes in my work place I had to make some amazing and also instructive experiences with some of my superiors. What was coming my way went beyond everything I had known. What was it about? I began to write a book about it in order to make it public. But what did I learn?

CAUTION!

"If you publish just one line about your work in a harmful sense, you will be dismissed without notice, and not even the labor union will be able to help you." This is about what a leading person from the staff board told me in private, and he went on: "Then you probably won't be able to find a job in the whole district of

Tübingen. Because the university's top persons all have seats in the supervisory boards of every private and public company." I had to swallow that. This means that, except for what I already said, I am not allowed to talk about my key experience, because then I would get to know the other side of our democracy which in this context is more reminiscent of East rather than West Germany.

Surely this first conflict had also to do with my personality, because on the one hand I was much too young and on the other hand I was much too hot-tempered; but the fact that I did not only feel like being bullied but as a victim of mobbing was certainly not my fault. Today I am more than grateful for this experience because it showed how, all of a sudden, an employee who had carried out his duties for 3 to 30 years and who maybe even identified with the company he worked for, can be thrown out onto the street with a kick in the ass, just because he does not fit anymore into the company's conceptions.

But still I liked my work at the university better than my work in the factory. Because in the course of time the emptying of garbage cans got less and less, and other tasks were added instead which offered far more variation than having to be standing in front of a machine the whole day.

In addition to my job at the university, my work as a writer and an editor was developing, too, and has provided a realistic goal ever since. Today I am perfectly aware that many employees do not have such a compensation in their everyday lives although everybody could profit from having a perspective which does not lead to resignation and which allows for looking to the future with hope.

POLITICAL CONCLUSIONS

During my year of vocational orientation in Reutlingen from 1979 to 1980 and also after my apprenticeship in Bad Urach from 1980 to 1983, my political and social interest increased more and more. My social interest was stirred by the books and reports by and about Günter Wallraff during my year of vocational orientation.

During my training as wood workman, peace politics were a central issue for me. Since then, it became more and more clear that I was going to refuse military service. Being a war orphan made me realize the disastrous effects a war can have and this is why joining military service, involving weapons, had become an unthinkable thing for me.

But I also became more and more aware of the fact that there was a lot of injustice in politics regarding to social issues. In that respect, I had already taken notice of the first social cuts in the support of the handicapped and of other people in social facilities during the old SPD government, cuts which were then perpetuated by the new CDU government after the so-called Bonn turn.

At trade school I had had a social studies teacher who was a convinced member of the FDP party. He passionately taught politics, much to classmates' dislike who were not particularly interested in politics. His teaching methods made me even more curious about politics. When he was standing at the blackboard telling us about democracy or governments in his vivid manner, I often liked to argue with him. He would patiently respond to my contributions trying to explain to me many interconnections; due to my stubbornness, however, this did not always work. In situations like these, many of my classmates would begin to moan when it had become too much for them again, but I did not care and I think that our teacher regarded that as a lively component of his teaching.

So it should not come as a surprise that my favorite subject was social studies.

At about that time, the Green Party was founded, and would remain a part of my political passion for a long time. Their peace politics and also their environmental issues were very appealing to me. But I also liked the rest of their party program which was still in the making then so that it was still possible to contribute to it. In addition, I also responded to their unconventional and refreshing attitude. The Green Party turned the gray political scenery of the 80s into something more colorful.

This is also what we need today, considering that 40% of our population are non-voters or protest voters: a new party which – like the Green Party did – would get rid of antiquated values providing a refreshing quality for society. Today's Green Party, however, is not suited for that role anymore because the party and its politicians, more often than not, are hardly different from the other parties, which cause as much enthusiasm for the young and elder citizens as a crash does for a stockholder. A new party that can get the people interested in politics again and will not become a right-wing threat is not to be seen yet. This should get our politicians to join in action as quickly as possible.

After my apprenticeship, my passion for politics became more anchored. In 1984 I became member of the Green Party. But before I had the guts to enter, I had to overcome some inferiority complexes first. The reason was that the Green Party was and continues to be a party characterized by its academic members. However, it used to be a lot more intellectual then and therefore too highbrow for me. One can imagine how I felt, having being a person with learning difficulties with nothing more to show than a intermediate school degree with special trade school training.

For the members of the Mössingen local party committee, where I was beginning to be active, I was a special case, but they were so open-minded that I finally became a member. The Mössinger Green Party were not as academically highbrow as was to be expected.

After joining them, I took part in every meeting and in countless election rallies of which there were quite a lot during that time of the Cold War. But I had great inhibitions to make verbal contributions during such events. For on the one hand I was not as eloquent as I would be later, and on the other hand I had to overcome my stage fright first, even if I was going to talk to a small group of only 10 people. So in spite of myself I began asking questions consisting of one or two sentences at the most, which was very little for a Green Party member then, considering that some members, after a five-minute monologue, had to be forced by the other members to finally ask their question. Things were quite chaotic anyway. Often it was just the loudest one who would be given the floor. To bring oneself to get one's way against all odds was more than a leap of faith. Later on I was known to ask short and concise questions and my brief and fitting comments on questions and contributions were quite popular with the people from the Green Party.

When I first opened my mouth at a nomination event in front of about 200 people, I fell flat on my face. Although my question was sensible, it should not have been asked at that point; I asked why they wanted by all means to nominate a woman as a regional candidate, since one does not vote for somebody just because they are a woman or a man. I would not vote for somebody just because

50

he is a worker or a handicapped person either. That was too much for the crowd and I was literally booed.

"Ouch!" – I had to swallow that. During the process of swallowing I realized that one should better think twice about what one is going to say and especially when and how one is going to say it. I read some books with political speeches which were not of much help as they all said the same. Books about rhetoric, on the other hand, were a real bonus. They taught you how to put across your convictions even when they were not very fashionable. But I had to realize that reading was one thing and reality quite another since things do not actually work out as theoretically logical as the books put them. So I decided to start by registering for adult evening classes in rhetoric for beginners in Tübingen. I was not surprised that I was the only non-academic person in the course. After all Tübingen is a university town. But the fact that the participants were or were going to be teachers, doctors, architects, lawyers, etc., who were struggling with the same problems like me, did indeed surprise me. For I had always thought that talking would be no problem for these people and that actually you already learn that at high school. But that just was not the case. The rhetoric course was big fun and every participant could talk freely without fearing to be booed or laughed at.
After that course I took part in several others which had to do with rhetoric and argumentation.

With every course I took, I became more and more assured, and not only was I able to handle my rhetoric better but also my body language. Now I virtually enjoyed making verbal contributions, in order to ask precise question or simply to make a statement. I also learned to play with it by either trying to make people boil with anger or cool them down with appropriate comments.

Slowly it dawned on me that politics has more to do with shows and games and very little with the average man in the street's everyday life.

When in 1990, at the first pan-German elections after the reunification, the Green Party was deservedly hardly voted for because it was ignoring social issues too much, I had a reason to really become politically active.

I must have covered several kilometers pacing my living room before I decided to run for regional candidate for the Tübingen district party committee of the Green Party in April 1992. I finally decided to take that step because I had demanded so many times myself that the Green Party should become more open to non-academic circles. And furthermore I was criticizing the fact that there were too few workers, i.e. non-academics, representing the interest of the people in the parliaments. So I thought why don't you do it yourself, because you cannot just recognize problems hoping that somehow they will disappear.

So again I had made up my mind to do something which was not easy to realize at all. But today I know that it was precisely that which attracted me: to do something new, to accept the challenge.

But to finally announce my candidacy officially was pretty frightening. For I had the feeling that someone like me running for that office will make a fool of himself. Finally I also had strong doubts whether I would not become unpopular in some circles and whether people with whom I had always gotten along fine might not turn their backs on me. For the Green Party had not the best of reputations then and was even considered as notoriously subversive. I wondered what my employer would think about my candidacy. For I was working for the state after all and the head of the university had no objective and critical attitude toward its own apparatus, and still has not. In addition, I belonged to a minority group and my focus on the integration of the handicapped was to be found in the platforms of neither the Green Party nor one of the other big parties.

When the evening had come when I was going to announce my candidacy at an annual meeting of the Mössingen local party committee, I drove there with my wife. Even 10 kilometers before reaching our goal, I was still struggling with my doubts and I asked my wife whether I should not rather destroy my application documents and forget all about it. But my wife replied as concisely and sensibly as always "You prepared everything so well that it would be a pity if you didn't pull it off."

I was relieved to find that my doubts were ungrounded. The party members were surprised, just like the local press that was present, but they found it appropriate that I was making an effort with my own focus on the integration of the handicapped and the opening of the Green Party toward non-academic circles. My application also drew encouragement from those I had had little or even nothing to do with.

And even people from all over the district party committee, which is characterized by heavy intellectualism, received the news of my candidacy with great encouragement.

The local press classified me as a surprise candidate because even insiders had not expected my candidacy. In addition, I turned out to be the very first person with former learning difficulties in the whole German political landscape to ever run for such a mandate.

However, my application also came as a surprise to my mother and siblings as well as everybody else I knew because I had not let anybody in on it except my wife. Today I know that that was the right decision because most would have considered me right away as being overenthusiastic and thus would only have confirmed my unjustified doubts; and so I would not have taken this important step which would later lead me on to many new paths.

At the nomination event I only got 8 votes out of a possible 72. However, it must be mentioned that there were three further male candidates and one female candidate. Among them Cem Özdemir, who got just two votes more and failed liked I did. Today Cem Özdemir is one of the best known politicians of Europe. He serves as an example for somebody who, having turned his own weaknesses into strengths and sporting idealism, ambition, strategy, his own issues and adaptability in politics as well as other areas in life, might reach a goal beyond his wildest dreams.

In the following years I ran three more times for an office like that. I never got elected but I accomplished what has always been the goal of my candidacies: to draw people's attention to issues and marginalized groups that hardly get mentioned or do not get mentioned at all.

So today I think that, if someone is honest and wants to reach the public with an important issue, a political party will provide an ideal platform for him or her. For there is hardly another area where one can draw so much media attention for one's cause. One gets the chance to reach a large part of the public one necessarily will have to address anyway in order to cause social change someday.

But if somebody really wants to get a fair chance of being elected, he or she has to stick to certain rules, like, for example, belonging to a large group within the party which has the right connections to the right people, something which can be difficult even on a regional level. In addition, one has to be obliging and reliable toward those people who are influential enough to be a help in gaining access to the political scene. Thus, it will be an advantage to hold one opinion now and another later. In short, one has to be reliable and must not try to pull one's own strings like the puppet called Pinocchio. The pulling of strings will lastly be accomplished by very few politicians, namely those who will hit the big time. And whether one is suited to that is a question one should ask oneself before being outmaneuvered.

Due to my political experiences and the hypocritical political behavior of the Green Party, I have already refused to make use of my right to vote, for I, too, have been increasingly wondering who to vote for when the parties hardly differ from another anymore, while predominantly those get to be in power who are primarily interested in their career. Thus, I have been distancing myself from politics more and more, without, however, finding it necessary to turn my back on it completely. Since, if more and more people did that and merely lived out their political commitment during tea-time, in the pub or in front of the TV, nobody should be surprised if someday all the social achievements if the last hundred years are wiped out in just ten.

STONY PATHS TO AUTHORSHIP

Although in 1989 I was only 25, I started writing my first autobiography. Usually you do not write your autobiography at that age but rather think about your future. But my recent past had been so moving and influential that I felt the need to immortalize those 25 years on paper, which helped me finally come to terms with a lot of things, too.

There are certainly many young people who have went through considerably more than I have. But unfortunately they seldom write about it. Books like that will be likely to provide more encouragement and advice than precocious publications by some experts who lack personal experience.

When in early 2000 several newspaper articles appeared about me, I got one of what have become countless telephone calls. It was a young woman who wanted to talk to me by all means. She came to see me and asked what to take care of when writing and how to write an autobiography. I replied that, before I could give her any good advice, I had to know what she wanted to write about first. So that 28-year old woman told me her life's story. Boy, oh boy. Compared to hers, my biography reads like one written by a naive, lucky child. That woman was put in a home by her parents when she was 3 years old and then an odyssey began through shared apartments and more homes. She was raped for the first time when she was 13 and was repeatedly taken care of by bad foster parents. She often ran away from her foster parents and struggled along on the street. Time and again, she was caught by the police and was sent either to a home again or to new foster parents. When she was 17, she got pregnant for the first time, by a former classmate who got her pregnant at a class reunion. He did not want to hear anything about that child and left her in the lurch.

Finally she brought herself to give her baby up for adoption. When she was 19, she got married for the first time and only realized after the wedding that her husband only felt good in women's clothes, which might have been tolerated, except that he regularly abused her sexually. Their marriage was sheer hell, and with 22, she got divorced for the first time. She began an apprenticeship and quit because of her bad marks in school, and began another which also failed. At 24 she got married for the second time. That marriage spawned two children. It broke up, too. Well, that woman told me lots more. What I found fascinating was that, in spite of everything, she has remained an optimistic woman with plans for the future.

I gave her some advice on how to approach her autobiography. If that woman managed to write it, I would publish it immediately, because, just like in my case, she did not live a life of high schools and universities, but her own life, and this is just what is most realistic.

But since, in spite of my dyslexia, I have been putting my thoughts to paper since the days of my apprenticeship, I did not want to write just another one of those countless sentimental autobiographies, but a book where I could put across my thoughts and my knowledge about the reasons for the exclusion of handicapped people in society. This is why I decided to describe only some extracts of my life and to combine them with topical texts.

One can imagine how virtually unsolvable the problem of writing was for me. But I took that as an additional challenge. My grammar was a catastrophe and so was my orthography. But due to the tireless help of my wife, I achieved some satisfying results with my texts. But technical advancement was of help, too. Although there were no affordable personal computers at that time, there were electronic typewriters with a memory of approximately 20 pages' worth and a one-line display. I scraped together 600 marks and bought a machine exactly like that. Since we were renovating our apartment at the time and my wife was pregnant, I finally had to borrow the money for the typewriter from the bank.

Today even good computer systems are affordable, which is very important for me, for, as I am wont to say, a computer with a good word processing program is as essential to me as a walking stick and a seeing-eye dog is for a blind person.

While I was writing, I realized more and more that I definitely had a lot of work ahead of me as regards my dyslexia. I took some further adult evening classes in German and orthography in Tübingen. While the reason for my first course of German was that I had to fill out packing slips at the factory and wanted to state my opinions in short letters to the editor, this time around the reason was that I really wanted to learn how to write properly, that is, as good as I my dyslexia allowed for.

When I was working in the factory, I had to fill out packing slips, and lest my colleagues noticed that I wrote damned badly, I always had a crib in my pocket and would secretly pull it out in order to see how you spell "drawer" or "plinth," etc.

It had been at least three years since my first course, and this time I took it to my stubborn head to write a book, which I also accomplished. When I had finished something, I did not know what to do with it. I just knew that it had to become a complete book in the end. But how? At least I knew that there were publishing companies and that was a start. So I asked information for some publishers' telephone numbers and started phoning them. I asked what I had to do with my written pages. Now I learned that there was something called manuscript and that it was precisely that which I was holding in my hands, and an editorial department that an author has to send his manuscript to in order to check if it is fit to be published. Then I learned that I had to choose the appropriate publishing companies in whose programs my book would fit in. So I started looking for publishing companies. After the 40th or 50th refusal, I gave up hope; most of the publishing companies would not publish my book because of economic reasons or because allegedly it did not fit into the companies' programs. A great many of them would have published it; however, only after receiving approximately 15,000 marks from me. Since I was naive but not stupid then, I thought that I could do that more cheaply on my own. I went to a copy shop in order to ask about production and costs. What they told me there sounded much more realistic to me. The costs for 150 copies were about 1,500 marks plus the costs for the printer's copy. That was already in 1991. Although there were computers with the necessary text processing programs, they were still expensive like hell. At the university they told me that there was an inexpensive typing agency which could transfer my manuscript into a computer file and also produce a model of the book on paper. I took that chance and paid another 2,000 marks for it. So it was not long before I finally had my first edition of 150 copies printed for 3,500 marks. The finished books arrived in cardboard boxes at the copy shop and I took them home by train. I was glad about it and as proud of it as a stag is after his first date. Yes, I even slept with by book. My amused wife just commented that I was a vainglorious guy, but I did not care because I had made it.

Now I had to go public. In order to do that I made use of my acquaintances in the press that I knew from my political work and contacted some appropriate journals. As if the press had been waiting for a biography like mine, tons of reviews followed. The local and national papers, too, released predominantly positive reviews. The reason was probably that I was the first author with a learning disorder in the German-speaking countries, and that my book had been written in an honest and informal manner which later would develop into my individual writing style, and which is characterized by the fact that I am not trying to desperately please anyone, but that I write in the same manner as I think, talk and act.

Today many authors ask me what I think of their manuscripts. Sometimes I answer that, although I like the manuscript, it reads like an essay at school. I try to explain two things to them: first, an author should write in his or her own style so that a reader who just reads a couple of pages knows immediately that it was written by that artist. And a writer should write about his or her own personal issues or else they will not differ from most of the rest, something which is indispensable considering the huge amounts of books being published.

But before I had developed my own style and, above all, before any authors started seriously asking me about my opinions, I had to go a long way of learning. In order to get closer to that goal, I decided to attend a two-year correspondence course on "How to Become an Author." Although the supervision of the homework was lousy, I thought that the choice of subject matter was very well balanced, and it served as an excellent introduction into the world of literature for me. I learned about all the different forms of literature and what matters most when writing in one or the other. I experimented to my heart's content and read several books' worth of reading recommendations that I found in the exercise books.

During that course I wrote my first novel Der Schicksalsschlag der Gesundheitsministerin [The Health Minister's Stroke of Fate] and my first novel for young people Sonderschüler Suppentrieler geht in die Schule und kann nichts?! [Sonderschüler Suppentrieler Goes to School and Can't Do a Thing?!]

By the way, the second novel is the first novel written for young people to focus on the issue of learning disorder; which is the reason for its success.

After that course there were two more correspondence courses, one in journalism and one in German.

I completed the course in German in January 1999 and got a D after all. In the written evaluation they told me that although my orthography was not the best, it would probably be sufficient for everyday correspondence. I thought about sending the teacher of the course, who had written the evaluation, the 15 books I had published by then, but that would have been too much for my Suabian economy.

Well, that was a sort of criticism I could accept, for I had become accustomed to hear things in a similar vein.

My first novel Der Schicksalsschlag der Gesundheitsministerin was torn to pieces by the critics so that I almost lost the courage to keep on writing. Today I have to admit that that criticism was legitimate, since even I decided to take it off the market because there simply were too many style errors typical for beginners.

But other new releases of mine as well got reviews that were not objective and where my texts were even attacked because of their spelling mistakes rather than their contents. Just imagine that: reviewers criticizing a dyslexic's spelling mistakes – presumably they even counted them. You could tell that according to some of the critics, I had better stay in the place intended for me by

Integration, like that tired old proverb "A cobbler should stick to his last."

As time went by, many critics also had a problem with me. While at first they still could label me as a "handicapped author," only few years later this was not possible anymore because I wrote about other minority groups, too, and not only e.g. specialized books or books for kids; I had fun writing in all genres. For I did not want to become just another run-of-the-mill author who always chooses the same form for the same contents. This would be comparable to a carpenter who saws out pegs with a jig saw all day long, although that craft is so versatile. But I also got very good reviews so that I had sleepless nights thinking that from now on things can only go downhill. I realized that it is not that easy to write really good reviews because in a good review, a book cannot be simply described as being either good or bad, but has to written about objectively.

Most of my readers, with whom I kept in contact at the beginning as they were only a few hundred, were not as unwilling to understand as some nagging critics were. Today however, my readers as well as my critics welcome the fact that my style has become more mature, the reason being that obviously writing books, too, has to learned first before one's own style gets broad recognition.

I did not only find recognition but also the job of my dreams: author and publisher. Without it I would not have got to know all those interesting people who have often inspired me to try something new.

BUMPY PATHS TO EDITORSHIP

After publishing my first book Für die Behindertenintegration, ein direkt Betroffener informiert in 1991 through my own publishing company, I found myself in a situation that was to change my life fundamentally.

The experiences with my own publishing company encouraged me to take the step from publisher of my own material to publisher proper. The difference is that in the former case a publisher only releases only his or her own material, and in the latter, mostly books by other authors.

Again I chose to do a mixture of both. The success of my first book gave me the motivation to write another one. So my first novel came about and had to be published, too. Again I looked for publishing companies in vain. So I had no other option than to publish my novel myself; after all I had gained some experience in that area. But since I was already working on my third book, it was clear that I would also want to publish that. I wondered whether it would make sense to offer the platform that I had created for myself to other authors as well. So it seemed natural to found my own publishing company I now had to find a name for. After thinking about it for a while, I decided to call it Mauer Verlag [Wall Publishing Company] with the following motto: "The publishing company where minorities write about minorities."

The name came about through the cover illustration for my first book showing simply a wall. A called that picture "Everybody wants to tear down some wall in their lives." This motto was to become the official slogan of my publishing company some years later.

With the founding of my publishing company I found myself a new forum, apart from politics, where I could support the needs of a "multicultural society of minorities," as I am wont to call it, including handicapped people, marginalized groups and social issues.

After I had come thus far, I had to get a trade license next, which was just a formality. The reason was that I would not be running my business in a strictly residential area, so there were no objections from the authorities with respect to the location. And since publishing companies which are that small usually do not have employees nor loud machines, there were no objections whatsoever from the Chamber of Industry and Commerce, the workmen's compensation board, the trade supervision board, the town clerk's office and all the other authorities which are usually the death of every German who wants to become self-employed.

Now my publishing company only needed a strategy. I designed a brochure where just my first three books were presented, with the note that the Mauer Verlag was looking for authors. Then I gathered up my contacts in the press and the radio and set about public relations in as relaxed and naive a manner as I had when founding my company. I made a point to make the best out of the means and knowledge that were at my disposal and to just let things develop. I still keep to that, if not as naively.

I got myself a press directory and noted down about 200 addresses where I sent a letter of information as well as the program of my company. That meant a lot of costs of materials. In addition, there were the production costs for my second and my third book, as well as the purchase of my used computer together with a wire printer. I also built a small bureau in the attic with the initial size of just 8 square meters. All that amounted to a total of 15,000 marks.

But I reckoned that that was still less money than a car would cost; and if I take its extras into account, they are about as expensive as the maintenance of my company (at least at the beginning). As a consequence, I sold my car.

When public relations began, who should call me but an editor of the local press in Tübingen. She said that my novel was intolerable and that she would not review it and that her colleagues shared that opinion (so do I by now). She even showed less understanding for my publishing company and said humiliating things about the program. She stated that only my own books were being presented in it, and that the note that I was looking for authors was nonsense, and that one just did not found a publishing company that way. She told me that I should first look for some authors and then found a publishing company. I just explained to her that I had to start somewhere and that my idea was right.

The feature about my company in the local papers after that telephone conversation was disastrous and I asked myself for the first time what kind of people critics are. Could it be that sometimes critics are trying to compensate for some repressed frustration in their lives or even that some of them are malicious idiots? But it was through that newspaper article that I found my first two authors, one female, one male, both from Tübingen. Later, a fruitful collaboration came out of this. Both released their debut through my company.

The female author was a former teacher of German, who had retired early, and quickly saw my weaknesses and my strengths at writing, and she could cope with my as yet immature writing style very well. She went through my texts for hours, charging me very little, so that I was able to learn a lot in addition to my correspondence courses and adult evening classes. The male author was the female author's partner, had found political asylum here and is a fantastic painter. He draw some cover illustrations for me at cost price.

When PR was well underway, dozens of articles appeared about me and my company and in contrast to the local press of Tübingen, they predominantly turned out to be rather good. The whole range in the press was represented, from the smallest journals to the national papers with the greatest circulation. Even magazines like the Neue Post, with a weekly circulation of 1,5 million copies, sent over a journalist and a photographer. Three months later, there followed an article in color which could not have been better. All that made me feel great because it meant that I had come through my baptism of fire, and I did not even burn my hands.

A short time afterwards, I went to the book fair to represent my company, which was like another baptism of fire. For I knew that I was lacking the professionality and that I was in danger of making a fool of myself. But my fears were completely groundless. Although there were some colleagues who smirked at me, most admired my courage and saw the potential of my commitment.

At the book fair, I also realized how varied the book industry is. Those eager to make money are as well represented as ingenious publishers and writers who focus more on the passion and the topic than on the business side. This behavior is exactly the reason for the demise of many publishing companies. I am still a publisher because of my love for literature, but I also quickly realized that the proceeds are essential if one wants to survive. For the book industry is not one bit different from other lines of industry, a fact which authors as well as some publishers just do not want to see. Neither do they like it if one tells them that they have to act like traveling salesmen selling vacuum cleaners or else their economic future will look rather bleak.

When I inherited a little money in 1997, keeping a mere 20,000 marks after paying back some debts and going on family vacation, my wife and I had to decide whether to invest the money in a car, in central heating or rather in a small book production system. I could convince my wife to buy a new professional digital copy machine and binding devices. I convinced her with the argument that it was not a fortune driving us to ruin in case we failed, and that a car would not be of much use when after 5 or 7 years it would only be worth a tenth of its original price. In contrast, with my own production system and sensible organization, I could contract as many writers as I wanted. And that exactly was the right decision.

I placed some advertisements in two important journals, saying that I was looking for authors, and within one year I contracted 12 new authors. And all the while the quality of the books' design was still comparable to that of a good book shop.

The first book I produced entirely on my own was a sheer catastrophe. The cover would arch, the text would partly slope and the pages were soiled, too. And as if that had not have been enough, the books fell apart.

But with every new book I produced, it got better. I signed more and more authors and orders were clearly increasing. I borrowed some money from the bank in order to supplement my production system with a bookbinding machine.

In order to become more professional, I developed a new company strategy which would turn out to be right. The motto of Mauer Verlag was now official: "Everybody wants to tear down some wall in their lives." Since I had to observe that a publishing company that has specialized too much is in a shaky situation, I settled on that new motto. I also observed that there are many authors that do not directly belong to a minority group, but who have nevertheless made a good literary contribution about it which is worth being published, even if it will reach only a small audience. So I decided that my company would be open to all writers and would accept all kinds of genres providing they focussed on minority and social issues. In 1998, the Mauer Verlag counted more than 50 authors.

Since technology has advanced so fast in so little time that now printing offices can produce books in good paperback quality for the same price as I can if I produce the books myself, I quickly rearranged production which gave my company additional impetus.

I reached a capacity that I could not manage anymore as a mere sideline. Due to the increasing amount of work to be done I could not do justice to my family and my friends anymore either. I had to choose whether to cut down my work either at my company or at the university. Since my job at the university was considerably less important, I decided to gradually reduce my working hours there. In addition, I passed on other publishing tasks to other companies so that I could take care of the management side of my company more thoroughly.

In 1998 I had 20 new releases, in 1999 there were 30, and in 2000 there were 40. So my initial idea developed into a small publishing company which is a mixture between a purely idealistic and a purely professional publishing company. With all the new authors as well as the marketing of my own persona and of Mauer Verlag, my company developed into a small publishing company in the German-speaking area that is gets respected and is appreciated by its authors.

FAMILY AND GOOD FRIENDS

Going to my regular disco in 1984, a girl attracted my attention more and more. Well, she was not exactly a girl anymore. She was 19 and I was 21 years old, and at that age you are already grown up after all. At the beginning I only observed her inconspicuously. She was shorter than me by a head and was not too slim, which I liked, had dark-blonde hair and some pimples in her face; I did not mind that, for I myself had just recently grown out of the age of pimples. She was dressed like most of the other young women in the disco were: relatively tight jeans and a shirt or blouse. To put it simply, she was completely to my taste, and even nowadays I enjoy looking at a woman like that. But with this young lady, looking was not going to be everything, I knew that much. I only needed a reason to talk to her without it seeming like a stupid come-on.

When I saw her at the Mössingen Christmas fair, where she was a saleswoman at a third-world stand, I finally found the right opportunity to talk to her. For at that time I was very much interested in politics, which of course includes aid to the Third World.

Since I have never been known to hesitate much, I immediately took my chances in our disco that same evening. We liked one another right away, but it was certainly not love at first sight. From that evening on, we would stand around close to another more and more often, and I realized that we felt attracted to each other. So I thought that it might be good if we started a relationship.

I have always been very suspicious of other people and did not like superficial friendships or relationships either. For even then I distinguished between a close friend and a friend, and I had enough friends. Close friends, however, I have had only a few. The difference is that a friend is more of a superficial acquaintance, or, for instance, a workmate, but a close friend is practically like a brother or like a wife. So I do not apply the word friend as loosely as many others who will call just about everyone their friend. These people do not seem to have understood what the word friend really means. It has been difficult for me to make friends since the days of my childhood, because I have been excluded too many times, and even by people who I thought were my friends.

I asked the young lady, whose name by the way is Friederike, whether we should try to have a close friendship. At first she hesitated or at least pretended to and after few minutes agreed with a long breathtaking kiss.

It was at the time when my professional future was still uncertain. I did not feel like working in the factory, in the line of work I had been trained in, and just needed time for orientation. So I could not avoid becoming unemployed every now and then. But what filled me with enthusiasm was politics and reading books about politics. Friederike soon got into it, too, and we went to countless political events from all political parties. We would passionately talk about political and social issues.

But it took some time before our friendship turned into love. Soon we also had the same big circle of acquaintances and a small circle of friends which brought us even closer together.

When my girlfriend finished her apprenticeship as a children's nurse in 1987, we got engaged. I did not want to at first, because I did not intend to get married since I thought that that just was not necessary, and I did not want kids either, because I thought that kids only made one dependent and that one becomes the family's slave. But Friederike just would not accept that, so one day

I thought, well alright, it does not matter anyway, for if two people love one another they might as well get married. One year after our engagement we had our marriage ceremony with everything that goes with it. It was a nice, corny party which even I liked.

Although we had bought an old apartment in Rottenburg shortly before we got married, we continued to live at my mother's house for a year. The reason was that we had to renovate our apartment first, which was a quite hard work and devoured a lot of money. But I saw to it that we did not get into debt too much and thus become absolute slaves of our propriety, which happens quite often with the Suabians. I have kept to this principle to this day and have managed to maintain a lot of independence. But nevertheless we suffered from lack of money after my wife had stopped working because she had gotten pregnant.

Half a year after our marriage an incidence occurred which deeply stirred me. My best man, who had been my best friend since the days of my childhood, committed suicide. My wife and I were devastated. Of course I was asking myself why he had done it, but also why he had not come to me with his vital questions. The only answer I found was that I simply had been too busy with my own life and thus could hardly be reached.

I decided that in the future I would take as much time for the few friends I have as is necessary in order to see them regularly.
Due to that devastating event it was even harder for me to make friends. In the past, every time I began to like a person too much, a wall would build itself up automatically inside of me reading "Stop! No trespassing!"

In 1990, when we were already living in our apartment, our life was enriched and particularly stimulated by the birth of our son.

Since I have always been full of ideas, and also crazy ones, we never got bored. Due to my activities, however, there were many periods where I had hardly time for my family. Today I try to see to it that my family gets sufficient attention and that we spend our time, which still is limited, at least intensely with each other, cultivating the friendships that we have.

TO GET A CHANCE OR TO TAKE IT

Due to the fact that I always developed further and set myself a new goal time and again, I achieved many things I would not even have dreamed of.

So with a lot of energy and effort I managed to escape the typical treadmill of a person with so-called learning difficulties. I did not achieve all that following a secondary or tertiary educational course, but my own. I realized that the secondary or tertiary educational course can often hold one's autonomy in check. For all too often I got to know people, educated people even, who, because of usual learning methods, had lost their personality. Often these people will not be able to do what they think is right; they might even not be capable of forming their own opinions.

By virtue of my autonomous educational path, I managed to turn my weaknesses into my strengths and to realize almost impossible things to my own surprise. As time went by, I became a role model for many people. This may sound like I was proud of my uniqueness, but this is not the case at all, on the contrary, it makes me sad, because I had to realize how hard it is as a member of a minority group to get a chance.

I am hearing all the time that you have to give a e.g. handicapped person or a member of another minority group a chance. But while searching for a publisher or trying to become established politically, it slowly dawned on me that these are just pretty words, and that you have to take your chance yourself. So it is clear to me now that if you hope for a chance as a minority, you have to take it in your own hands and must not wait until somebody hands it to you. That is why I am a strong believer in "helping someone to help themselves."

During my PR work I had to learn again and again that the media, too, will only give you a real chance if you already achieved something, simply if you have built yourself up on your own. The following example shall serve as an illustration. In 1991 I decided to participate in the annual Christmas event hosted by a regional news show of the Südwestfunk television network, naively believing that honest commitment is all that counts. I sent a very sympathetic letter to the network's address. In that letter I suggested that I would donate 5 marks of every sold copy of my first book Für die Behindertenintegration, ein direkt Betroffener informiert, which I had released the same year. And would you believe it, a gentleman from the production office called me up to tell me that my idea was very laudable and that a camera crew would come to see me in the next couple of days in order to shoot a documentary about me.

I was overjoyed with all that appreciation. But only 3 days later, the same gentleman called again telling me that they had changed their mind. I started thinking: My name is not Boris Becker, so I can't auction off my tennis racket for a lot of money; I'm not a rock star either, who could auction off his sweaty shirt for a small fortune; and I'm not the owner of a fashion company worth millions, who could sell a piece of clothing for 5,000 marks in order to get a 3-minute ad-like documentary for regional television in return. That example taught me that only people who either can buy into it with their money, or who have already worked their way up to some extent, can use the mass media for their purposes.

So much for the chances the media can give you. The following two concluding examples may serve as an illustration of the chances somebody gets if he or she lacks the necessary education.

If I applied for a job as an editor at some newspaper today, I would very probably lose out because I simply do not have the necessary educational documents. Presumably it would not even matter that

I have already published about 20 books and that I am running my own publishing company with economic success.

The second example: In 1995 I applied for a job as a public relations officer at an association for social issues. Of course I lost out. If I applied for that job today, they would probably also employ somebody who meets the requirements of having studied an appropriate subject. And it would not matter much that I have become an authority, as it were, with respect to public relations work, as my own build-up work has shown.

THE MULTICULTURAL MINORITY SOCIETY – JUST A DREAM?

When I started to become active politically, I focussed primarily on the integration of the handicapped. After all, this social milieu is where I have my roots. However, as time went by I realized that the needs of the handicapped are the same as those of other marginalized groups. This is why I conceived a new societal concept, which I called "multicultural minority society." In that context I published the book Mutige Wege zur multikulturellen Minderheitengesellschaft [Brave Paths toward a Multicultural Minority Society]. That book tied in with my very first publication Für die Behindertenintegration, ein direkt Betroffener informiert. In my books Mut zu Lampsacus, die multikulturelle Minderheitengesellschaft [Courage in Lampsacus, the Multicultural Minority Ssociety] from 1998 (in collaboration with Otto Rössler) and Mutige Wege zu einer humanen Welt [Brave Paths toward a Humane World] from 2000 I delved deeper into the issue of a multicultural minority society (henceforth, MMS). Through these book publications and my political work, I managed in the course of time to establish the idea of MMS more and more.

Now I am going to shift my style a little and focus on MMS for a while because the realization of MMS has become an essential part of my life, and therefore it will not be disruptive to my autobiography, on the contrary, it will probably make my it more interesting, since the idea of MMS is based on my own life experiences.

A VERY LARGE CONCEPT

Every group of people may call themselves a "minority" nowadays. Sometimes that word is misused. This may happen, for instance, when some wing of a political party is more on the left, right, or somewhere in between, and thus calls itself a minority; or when some people momentarily take advantage of including themselves in this or that minority in certain situations.

What can count as a minority? According to the Brockhaus lexicon, a minority is "within a society a group that consists of a smaller amount of members than the rest. In democratic countries, it is the will of the majority which is valid. In order to secure the freedom and equality of everyone, minorities will often be protected by the constitution, or the law; valid decisions (e.g. constitutional changes) will require a qualified majority by means of introducing the system of proportional representation or other minority rights. The third article of the constitution furthermore prohibits discrimination of members of a minority."
Furthermore, it says:
"According to international law, a minority is a group of members of a nation, who by virtue of their heritage, language, religion or culture differ from the majority of the nation's people and who form a certain social unit within society. In order to grant protection to such a minority, special legal measures will often be necessary, such as the acknowledgment of their language as a second official language, the establishment of minority schools and the permission for limited self-government."
As regards social minority groups, the Brockhaus lexicon states:
"Social minority, a partial group within a comprehensive society that differs from the ruling majority and the values, norms and properties this majority considers as valid, by virtue of existing (polyethnic, confessional, linguistic, racial, cultural) characteristics.

The minority as an excluded group is often subject to social prejudice and discrimination (also the role of a scapegoat) by the majority." So much for the Brockhaus lexicon.

Which social groups belong to minorities?
The best-known are: handicapped people, gays, lesbians, foreigners, foreign workers, asylum seekers, ethnic resettlers, chronic patients, religious people, Romanies, unemployed people, recipients of social security benefits, disadvantaged elders, abused children, oppressed women, the so-called 'new man,' psychologically unstable people and overweight people. I better stop now since this list would have to be more than twice as long.

Oh well, even millionaires, which represent about 5% of the German population, might count as a minority. It should not be left unsaid, however, that these few millionaires hardly belong to the group of disadvantaged people in society. For their capital influences the economy and politics so much that they seem to be the ones in power, something which all the economic and political scandals have increasingly proven during the last years.

Often, minorities are termed differently, like e.g. a small part; few; a few; not many; inferior people; failures; degenerate; not fitting; freaks; children of Satan; fucked up; bad; evil; contaminated; dangerous; unworthy, etc. What is striking with this list is that it is only a small part of the whole range of possible terms and that I left out the really devastating words, like e.g. ethnical cleansing, euthanasia, not worth being alive...

So it makes sense to explain why in the future one must not talk about a multicultural society, but a multicultural minority society. In my eyes, a multicultural society means that several cultures and peoples live together in peace, as human behavior permits, in a country or a community of nations like Europe, and learn from one another; every people respects the other people's culture and religions, and none of them present themselves as superior.

One might ask what all these minorities, or marginalized groups, have in common. It is clear that every marginalized group involves both pain and pleasure. Another thing they have in common is that the public presents them as strange or even threatening, which might stigmatize them as outsiders, given contemporary circumstances or the political situation. This can lead to persecution, torture and mass murder of one or several minority groups by a goaded majority of the population. In order to prove this, one does not even have to look at the Third Reich or look further back in time; recent history is alarmingly sufficient for that purpose considering, for instance, former Yugoslavia, Iran, Ireland, the persecution of the Curds, etc.

In spite of all these terrifying facts, what counts is that all minorities, whether in Germany or in other countries, have one thing in common: they want to be accepted the way they are and not be coerced into an adapted lifestyle, something which all marginalized groups can jointly achieve. In this respect, it is important that the individual minorities do not let themselves be divided by their own representatives, which often happens through politics and economy due to materialism and obsession with power. For it may be quite convenient for the powers that be when one or several minorities (peoples and cultures) start fighting with each other, because then the mob will neutralize itself, while those in power will have the necessary calmness to follow their political as well as political interests.

In the future, it must not be possible anymore to make observations like the following: a so-called anti-social person complains about a Turk, and the Turk complains about the anti-social person; or a foreign worker curses an asylum seeker; or an unemployed person thinks that he is entitled to be unemployed, but that the rest of the unemployed people are just lazy. These situations are not made up at all; unfortunately they are omnipresent.

Therefore the long-term goal to be reached must be that all minority groups become united so that they jointly stand up for the ideal that no persons, peoples or religions, nor nations consider themselves as superior. And it must be irrelevant how much of a financial burden a minority society causes, or, to put it in typically German fashion, how much prosperity must be given away. For peace among people is worth more than money, money, money.

Unfortunately, one often hears other leading industrial nations, too, say: "It is easy to talk about sharing when you haven't got anything to share yourself and just keep your hands open."

Surely much of what I have written in this chapter sounds utopian or even ridiculous.
But it isn't!
For we only have to take a look at our past and we will be surprised at how many possible and formerly impossible things have been achieved during the last 100 years alone!

80

UPS AND DOWNS, OR WHAT DOES 'FUTURE' MEAN ANYWAY?

I have several ideas and goals for the future so that I will certainly not get bored in the next years.

One goal is to reduce my social commitment to a certain extent compared to the past years. It just would take too much power. For in spite of my young age there were simply too many ups and downs. Or what does "in spite of my young age" mean anyway? After all, as I am writing this autobiography, I am not even 40 years old, but still this is pretty much. I realized that during the shooting of a 30-minute SWR television documentary about me.

When on a Saturday afternoon the last scenes of the film were shot at my old school and there was a short break, I took the opportunity to walk into my old classroom. There I sat at my old desk, and thought about the fact that I could not have been more than 9 years old when I once sat there. That is when I realized how old I really am. After all there were almost 30 years in between. I knew that compared to a 70 or even 80-year old I am still quite young, but on the other hand I have definitely reached half-time and have been through more than many other persons of the same age or even considerably older than me. I realized that that might be exactly what made me so interesting for television and for many people.

Due to my experiences in life, I have made up my mind for the future to defend myself against any kind of labeling, which deprives every single person, regardless of their age or social stratum, of their freedom to do what is beneficial to their intellectual and physical development.

Since the end of my school years, or rather of my apprenticeship, I have achieved many things others never thought possible. But I am completely aware of the fact that I may lose rather quickly what I have gained. For instance, not so long ago I had some trouble with my employer and could even have lost my job. Also, my publishing company and my writing was not yet doing well financially. So it would not have taken much more and a lot would have ended up differently.

However, I also want to keep one thing for the future, and that is my reflection in the mirror; the fact that, with respect to all the things I have done, I can still look me in the eye without having to lie to myself.

When I was young I very often used up my energy due to a false optimism and generally misjudged people's good will. Very often, I focussed much too little on my private life and also cared too little about myself; by now I have learned that a certain amount of egotism is not bad at all.

My commitment as publisher and writer will be as important as my private life. The building up of young and older authors with social issues in particular is close to my heart. In that respect, I hope that my publishing company may serve as a stepping-stone for authors of that kind so, with their important issues, they might get people to think and maybe even to take action.

I know that in case my degree of popularity should increase further, I have to try hard not let it go to my head lest I become arrogant (I hate nothing more than conceit and arrogance), so that my readers as well as my sympathizers may continue to identify with my work.

So my readers and sympathizers can be sure to expect a lot from me. But it hardly makes sense just to talk about ideas, because, in the end, you have to realize them on your own. But a lot will come to nothing, too, and before you know it you stand there like a charlatan, or even in front of a void. But also, talking about ideas will not do because my experience taught me that it is hardly possible to make plans for your future. It is even probable that making plans for the future is just a sign for repression of reality, since modern developments or the suffering of a blow like e.g. a shock, an accident or a new challenge, may knock everything that had been planned on the head.

During my hot-tempered and extremely energetic years, I wanted not only to plan 10 steps in advance, but to take them immediately, too. But time taught me that it makes more sense to plan just 2 or 3 steps in advance at the most, and that it is best to let every single step come to you.

Number One Niche Market Author in the German-Speaking Area

Wilfried Kriese's motto: To turn one's weaknesses into one's strengths

Wilfried Kriese's books distinguish themselves through their unusual issues and varied literary forms. With his extraordinary topics, he has managed to establish himself as the number one niche market author.

This is due to works like e.g. Meine Wolle Kriwanek Story, Halbzeit – die eigenen Schwächen zu Stärken machen, Käse statt Zinsen, Familie Haus Arbeit Auto CityEL, Lebenswege das Generationen Computerspiel, In meinen Augen Günter Wallraff, Mut zurMultikulturellen Minderheitengesellschaft, etc.

With his 1991 book Für die Behindertenintegration – ein direkt Betroffener informiert, he was the first person in Germany with a previous learning disorder to become a book author.

The common thread running through his books are social issues and marginalized groups, just as it has throughout his life as formerly linguistically and cognitively handicapped person and dyslexic. He spent all his school-years in special schools for mentally challenged children. After school, Kriese did not follow a secondary or tertiary educational course, but his own.

Wilfried Kriese's writing style is characterized by the fact that he is not trying to desperately please anyone, but writes in the same manner as he thinks, talks and lives.

After 15 years of literary work and 20 published books, Wilfried Kriese has become the number one niche market author in the German-speaking area.

His works have become a mirror of society and documents of historical import.

Due to its focus and its selected books, his publishing company Mauer Verlag, founded in 1992, developed into a respected small publishing house in the German-speaking area.

Wilfried Kriese and his Mauer Verlag have become known through newspapers, radio and television.

Get more information through:
www.mauerverlag.de / www.plattformverlag.de / www.wilfried-kriese.de

THE CURRENT SITUATION

The text in this book has been taken from the autobiography Half-Time, published in 2001.

In the meantime, a lot has been happening, you can get an update on current activities at www.wilfried-Kriese.de!

The Wilfried Kriese Edition 2003

This program offers a large selection of Wilfried Kriese's varied literary work. The books have been numbered according to the order of their publication.
This program illustrates how a writer's style may develop and become firm in the course of time.

Wilfried Kriese's writing style is characterized by the fact that he is not trying to desperately please anyone, but writes in the same manner as he thinks and talks.

The common thread running through all of Wilfried Kriese's books as well as his publishing company Mauer Verlag, which he founded in 1992, is the preoccupation with social issues and marginalized groups. In that way, his works have become a mirror of society and documents of historical import.

This edition was published in 2003 on the occasion of the 15-year anniversary of Wilfried Kriese's literary career.

1. Für die Behindertenintegration – ein direkt Betroffener informiert [For the Integration of the Disabled – Information by a Directly Affected Person] Biography/nonfiction.
2. Der Schicksalschlag der Gesundheitsministerin [The Health Minister's Stroke of Fate] Novel.
3. Sonderschüler Suppentrieler geht in die Schule und kann nichts (?!) [Sonderschüler Suppentrieler Goes to School and Can't Do a Thing?!] Youth novel.
4. Freie Gedanken [Free Thoughts] Poetry.
5. Mut zur Multikulturellen Minderheitengesellschaft [Brave Paths toward a Multicultural Minority Society] Nonfiction/biography.
6. Was – Auf der Suche nach einer Welt ohne Namen [What – In

Search of a World Without Name] Fairy tale.

7. rotstift oder normen normen normen [red crayon, or norms norms norms] 43 illustrations, poetry.

8. Haarsträubende Machtmißbräuche von Vorgesetzten – Täter und Opfer [Hair-raising Abuses of Power by Superiors – Culprits and Victims] Nonfiction.

9. Brunos Freiflug nach Kenia [Bruno's Free Flight to Kenya] Satire.

10. Mutige Wege zu einer humanen Welt [Brave Paths toward a Humane World] Nonfiction.

11. Gerechtigkeit für Rösslers [Justice for the Rösslers] Nonfiction.

12. Hoffnungs Freiflug nach Bali [Hoffnung's Free Flight to Bali] Satire.

13. Halbzeit – die eigenen Schwächen zu Stärken machen [Half-Time – to Turn One's Strengths into One's weaknesses] Biography.

14. Käse statt Zinsen – die Alpe Sonnhalde, von der Vision zum Erfolg [Cheese instead of Interest – Sonnhalde, from Vision to Success] Report.

15. Familie Haus Arbeit Auto CityEL [Family Home Work Car CityEL] Satire.

Schwäbisches Tagblatt (8.8.2003) People in the news

The best-known (and confessed) dyslexic from Rottenburg has recently been allowed to call himself "Dr. h. c." (doctor honoris causa). The author and publisher Wilfried Kriese, age 40, has been awarded this honorary degree at an international convention in Baden-Baden last week on the behalf of an institute of the Canadian University of Windsor (Ontario). Computer scientist George E. Lasker, the head of the institute, published the English version of Lampsacus, issued five years ago by Kriese and the Tübingen chaos scientist Otto E. Rössler. Among other things, that book discussed the way that the internet can contribute to worldwide communication among minority groups. According to Kriese, he received the title for his "outstanding achievements, exemplary pedagogical leadership and outstanding services to mankind:"